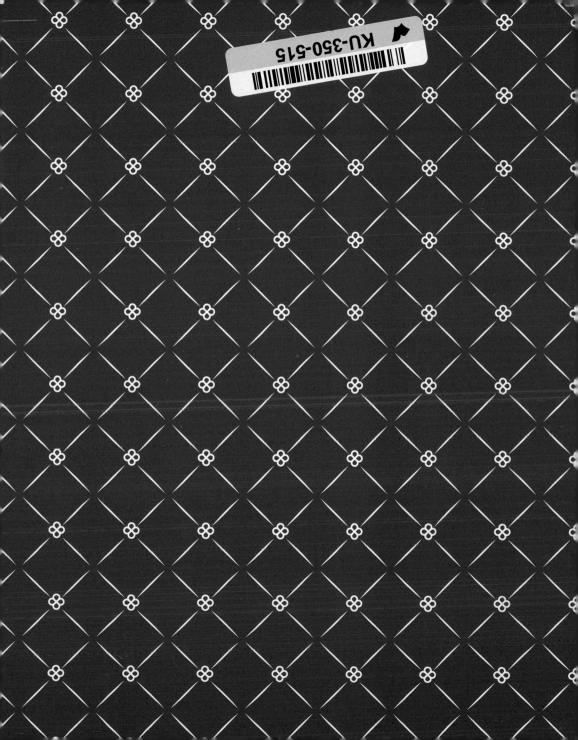

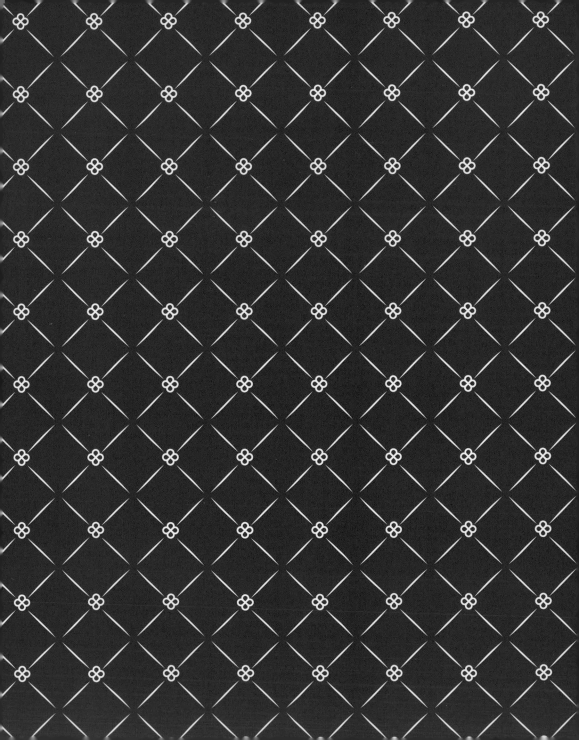

This book belongs to

_____

_____

This edition published by Parragon Books Ltd in 2015

Parragon Books Ltd
Chartist House
15–17 Trim Street
Bath BA1 1HA, UK
www.parragon.com

ISBN 978-1-4748-0637-4

Printed in China

Disney·PIXAR MOVIE COLLECTION

A CLASSIC DISNEY STORYBOOK SERIES

Cars

Bath · New York · Cologne · Melbourne · Delhi
Hong Kong · Shenzhen · Singapore · Amsterdam

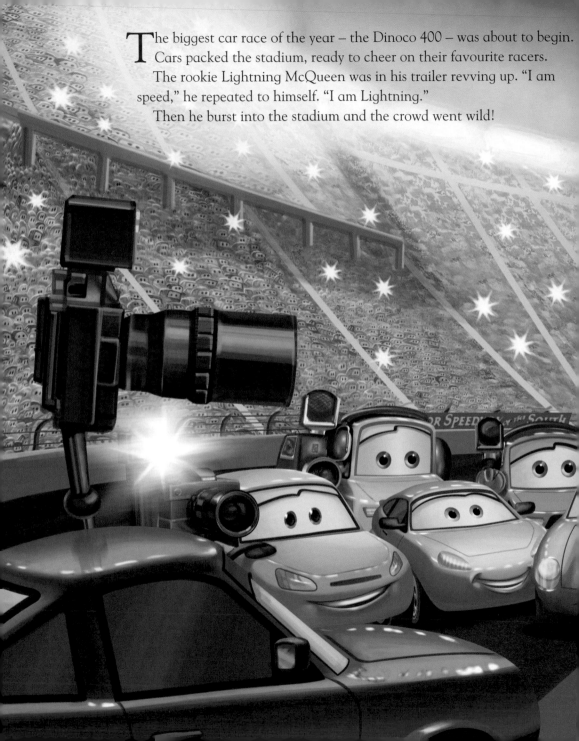

The biggest car race of the year – the Dinoco 400 – was about to begin. Cars packed the stadium, ready to cheer on their favourite racers.

The rookie Lightning McQueen was in his trailer revving up. "I am speed," he repeated to himself. "I am Lightning."

Then he burst into the stadium and the crowd went wild!

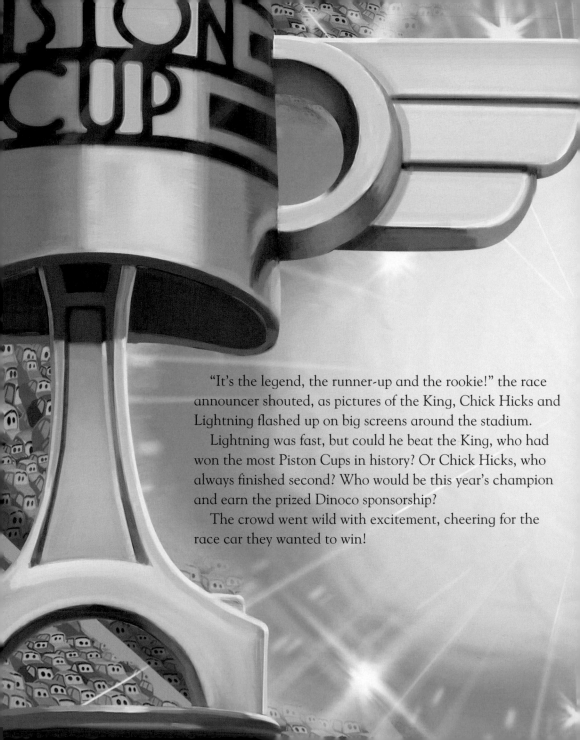

"It's the legend, the runner-up and the rookie!" the race announcer shouted, as pictures of the King, Chick Hicks and Lightning flashed up on big screens around the stadium.

Lightning was fast, but could he beat the King, who had won the most Piston Cups in history? Or Chick Hicks, who always finished second? Who would be this year's champion and earn the prized Dinoco sponsorship?

The crowd went wild with excitement, cheering for the race car they wanted to win!

VA-RRoom! Soon the cars were off and racing. Lightning and Chick Hicks sped round the track side by side.

Suddenly, Chick slammed into Lightning, sending him skidding off the track.

Engine roaring, Lightning raced to catch back up –
only to face a huge pile-up, caused by Chick!

"Get through that," Chick muttered as he headed
in for a pit stop. Amazingly, Lightning raced between
the wrecked cars and leaped into the lead!

But while the rest of the racing cars went to the pits,
Lightning kept going....

Lightning had made a huge mistake! On the last lap ...
BANG! BANG! His two rear tyres blew out!

As he limped towards the finish line, the King and
Chick caught up. Lightning stuck out his tongue to gain
an edge, but it was too close to call.

While waiting for the final result, Lightning boasted
to the reporters, "I'm a one-man show."

"We quit!" His insulted pit crew stormed away.

"You need to wise up and get yourself a good team,"
the King told him.

But Lightning wasn't listening. He was too busy
daydreaming about fame and fortune....

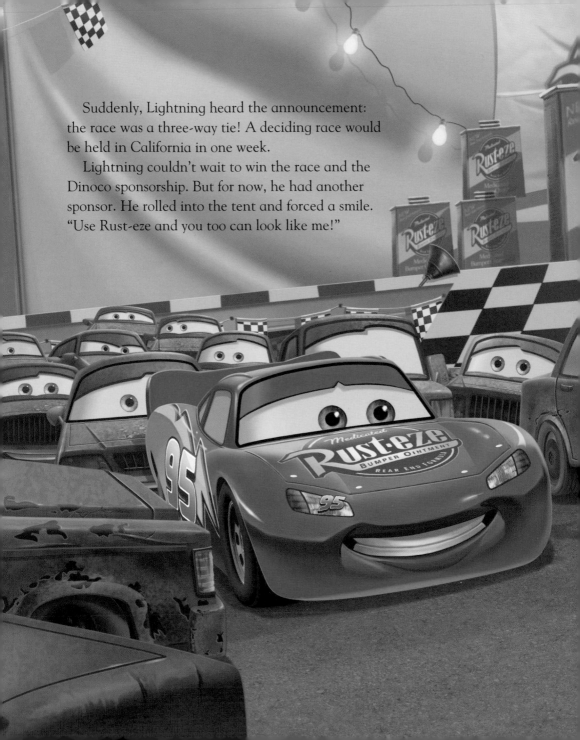

Suddenly, Lightning heard the announcement: the race was a three-way tie! A deciding race would be held in California in one week.

Lightning couldn't wait to win the race and the Dinoco sponsorship. But for now, he had another sponsor. He rolled into the tent and forced a smile. "Use Rust-eze and you too can look like me!"

Many long hours later, Lightning's driver, Mack, needed to get some sleep.

"We're driving all night," Lightning insisted.

As Mack struggled to stay awake, four flashy cars pulled alongside and pushed him back and forth across the road. Startled awake, Mack swerved dangerously....

Lightning, asleep in the back, rolled out and awoke to the
sight of traffic racing towards him on the Interstate.

Terrified, Lightning looked for Mack. He thought he saw
him going down an exit ramp and quickly followed. But it wasn't
Mack – he was lost on the old Highway 66!

Suddenly he heard a loud siren and saw red lights flashing.
A sheriff was after him! Lightning raced away fast.

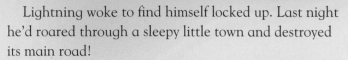

Lightning woke to find himself locked up. Last night he'd roared through a sleepy little town and destroyed its main road!

"My name's Mater," a friendly tow truck said.

"Where am I?" Lightning asked.

"Radiator Springs!" Mater replied proudly.

Just then, the sheriff arrived. It was time for Lightning to go to court.

The courthouse was filled with upset and angry townsfolk.

"Make him fix the road," Sally, the town lawyer, told the judge. Sally said that without a road, there would be no travellers and no business for the town.

The judge, Doc Hudson, made his ruling: Lightning couldn't leave until he had fixed the road.

Lightning pulled Bessie, the road-paving machine, down the road as fast as he could. Sticky tar splashed everywhere and when it dried, the road was uneven and bumpy.

When Mater drove down the road, every nut and bolt in his body rattled!

"It looks awful!" exclaimed Sally.

"Now it looks like the rest of the town," Lightning replied rudely.

Insulted, Doc stared long and hard at Lightning. Then he challenged the young hotshot to a race. "If you win, you go. If I win, you do the road my way," he said.

Lightning agreed. He was sure he could beat the old car.

Out at the dirt track, Lightning took a quick lead, leaving Doc in a cloud of dust. But when he made a sharp turn, he lost control and skidded into a cactus patch.

"You drive like you fix roads," said Doc. "Lousy."

Humiliated, Lightning went back to work.
The next morning, the townsfolk awoke to a smooth new road.
Even Doc was impressed.
But where was Lightning?

He was practising the turn he'd missed when he had raced Doc.
Watching Lightning miss the turn again, Doc offered some advice:
"You've got to turn right to go left."
Lightning just laughed. What did Doc know about racing?

Giving up on the turn, Lightning returned to the town all dusty.
He found that the townsfolk had begun to spruce up their shops.
  Suddenly, Red, the fire engine, sprayed water on Lightning.
  "If you want to stay at the Cozy Cone, you've got be clean," Sally said.
She owned the motel and thought that Lightning might like to stay there.
Sally was starting to like him and the effect he was having on the town.
  "You're being nice to me!" a surprised Lightning said.

That night, Mater showed off his backwards driving.

"Maybe I'll use that technique in my big race," Lightning said. "I'll be the first rookie in history ever to win it. I'll get a big new sponsor with private helicopters...." Lightning even promised Mater a helicopter ride.

"I knowed I made a good choice," Mater told Lightning.

"A good choice about what?"

"My best friend," said Mater. Lightning smiled as Mater drove away.

When Lightning drove to Sally's motel, he discovered that she had overheard the conversation.

"Did you mean it? That you'll get him a helicopter ride?" she asked.

"Oh, who knows?" Lightning said casually.

Sally turned to leave. "Mater trusts you," she said, frowning.

"Thanks for letting me stay here!" Lightning added quickly.

"Goodnight," Sally replied.

The next morning, while Lightning was waiting for his daily fuel ration, he wandered into Doc's back garage.

And then he saw it: a grimy old Piston Cup. The plaque read, *The Hudson Hornet, Champion: 1951.*

There were Piston Cups from 1952 and 1953, too.

Lightning couldn't believe it. Doc was a racing champion!

When Doc found Lightning, he was furious. "The sign says, *stay out!*"

"You're the Hudson Hornet! You still hold the record for most wins in a single season!" Lightning babbled.

"All I see is a bunch of empty cups," Doc grumbled as he pushed Lightning outside and then slammed the garage door.

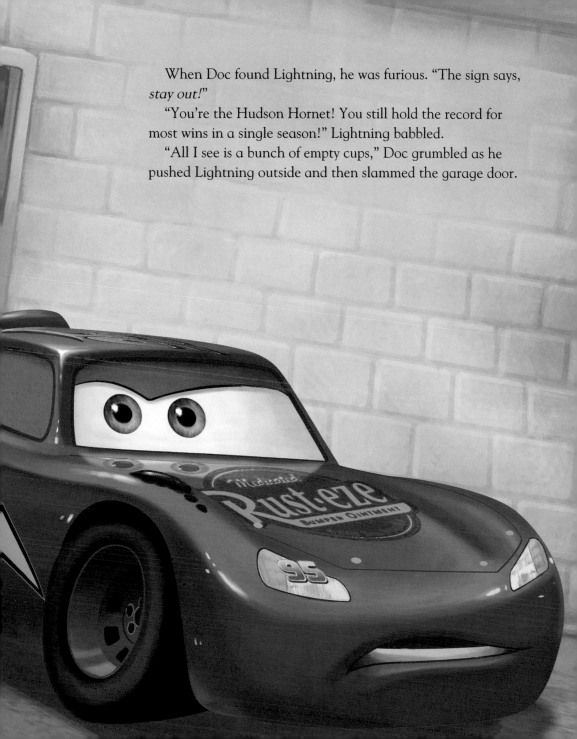

Bursting with excitement, Lightning told everyone in town about Doc. But they all thought he was crazy.

That was when Sally arrived and gave Lightning a full tank of fuel. Lightning could have sped out of town, but instead, he happily drove with Sally through the beautiful mountains.

"The Wheel Well Motel," Sally said, showing Lightning an empty building. "It used to be the most popular stop on Highway 66."

Then Sally told him that she was once a big-shot lawyer in Los Angeles. On a drive across the country, she'd landed in Radiator Springs. It was the first time she had truly felt like she was home.

Sally explained that the big Interstate outside town hadn't always existed. Before it, Highway 66 had been the main road.

"Back then cars didn't drive on it to make great time – they drove on it to have a great time. Then the town got bypassed just to save ten minutes of driving," Sally sighed. "One of these days we'll find a way to get back on the map."

Later that afternoon, Lightning spotted Doc wearing racing tyres at the dirt track.

Ducking out of sight, the rookie watched Doc race effortlessly round the tricky curve that had given Lightning so much trouble.

"Wow! You're amazing!" exclaimed Lightning. "How could a car like you quit at the top of your game?" he asked.

"You think I quit? They quit on me," Doc replied bitterly.

Lightning listened as Doc told him about his big crash. When Doc had recovered, he'd been replaced by a rookie – a rookie like Lightning.

The next morning, a new main road stretched from one end of Radiator Springs to the other.

"Good riddance," muttered Doc, happy that the racing car appeared to have finished the job and left town.

But Lightning hadn't left. Instead, he became the best customer Radiator Springs had seen in a long time! He got new tyres, some of Fillmore's organic fuel, supplies at Sarge's, bumper stickers at Lizzie's and a paint job at Ramone's.

"What do you think?" Lightning asked, surprising Sally with his makeover.
"It looks like you've helped everybody in town," Sally said gratefully.

On Lightning's cue, the shopkeepers turned on their newly fixed neon
signs – just as they had done in Radiator Springs' heyday.

It was time to cruise! Everyone drove happily and slowly up and
down the street. It all seemed close to perfect ...

... until a wall of headlights approached.

"We have found Lightning!" boomed a voice from a helicopter. Reporters swarmed the small town.

"I'm sorry I lost you, boss," Mack said. And on Mack's speakerphone, Lightning's agent, Harv, told him to get to the race fast!

Pushing through the crowd, Lightning found Sally. But he didn't know what to say.

"I hope you find what you're looking for," Sally told him. Then she turned and disappeared into the crowd.

"Sally!" Lightning called after her, but it was too late.

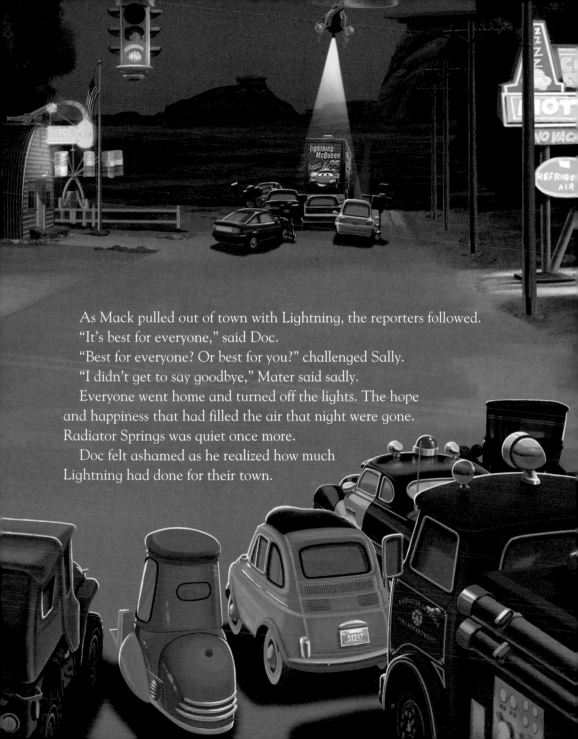

As Mack pulled out of town with Lightning, the reporters followed.
"It's best for everyone," said Doc.
"Best for everyone? Or best for you?" challenged Sally.
"I didn't get to say goodbye," Mater said sadly.
Everyone went home and turned off the lights. The hope
and happiness that had filled the air that night were gone.
Radiator Springs was quiet once more.
Doc felt ashamed as he realized how much
Lightning had done for their town.

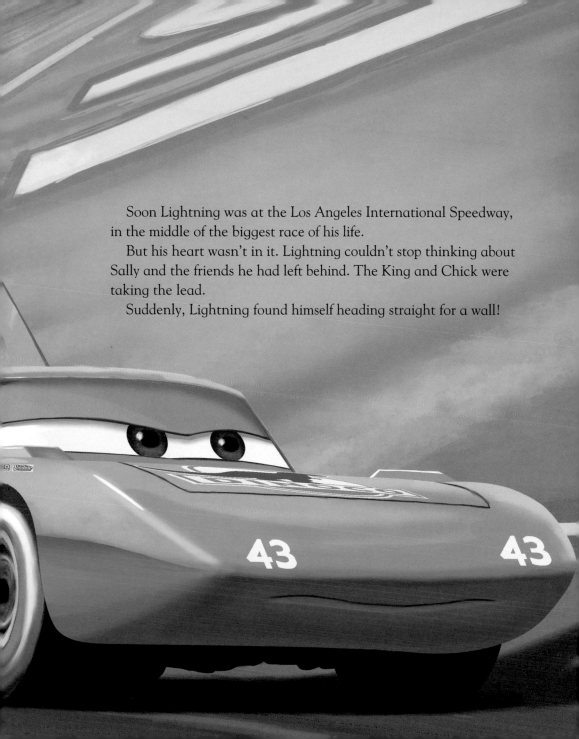

Soon Lightning was at the Los Angeles International Speedway, in the middle of the biggest race of his life.

But his heart wasn't in it. Lightning couldn't stop thinking about Sally and the friends he had left behind. The King and Chick were taking the lead.

Suddenly, Lightning found himself heading straight for a wall!

As he recovered from his near miss, Lightning heard a familiar voice over his radio. It was Doc!

All of Lightning's Radiator Springs friends had come to be his crew! And when the fans saw that Doc – the fabulous Hudson Hornet – was the crew chief, they gave a roaring cheer.

Doc focused on Lightning. "If you can drive as good as you can fix a road, then you can win this race with your eyes shut!" he shouted.

Lightning took off with new determination. When Chick bumped him off the track, he used the 'turn right to go left' trick. He even drove backwards, like Mater!

But just as he was about to cross the finish line and win, he looked back and saw that Chick had caused the King to crash.

As Chick won the race, Lightning sped back to the King.
"What are you doing, kid?" Doc asked through the headset.
"I think the King should finish his last race," Lightning answered as
he pushed the racing car over the finish line. The crowd cheered loudly.
Chick had finally won his Piston Cup, but the fans booed him!

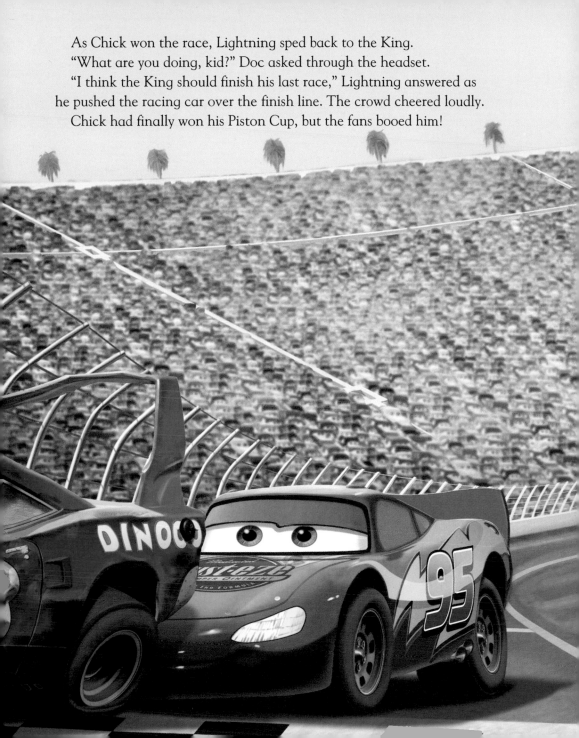

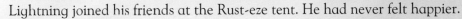

Lightning joined his friends at the Rust-eze tent. He had never felt happier. When Tex, the owner of Dinoco, asked, "How'd you like to become the new face of Dinoco?" Lightning graciously said no. He'd decided to stay loyal to the Rust-eze gang, who had believed in him from the beginning.

He did ask Tex for one small favour, though....

Back at the Wheel Well, Sally was looking out over the valley when she heard a voice say, "I hear this place is back on the map."

It was Lightning! "There's a rumour floating around that a hotshot Piston Cup racing car is setting up his big racing headquarters here."

The two cars smiled happily at each other.

That was when Mater came flying by – in a Dinoco helicopter!

"Well, he is my best friend," Lightning said, laughing.

Sally smiled. Lightning was home at last.

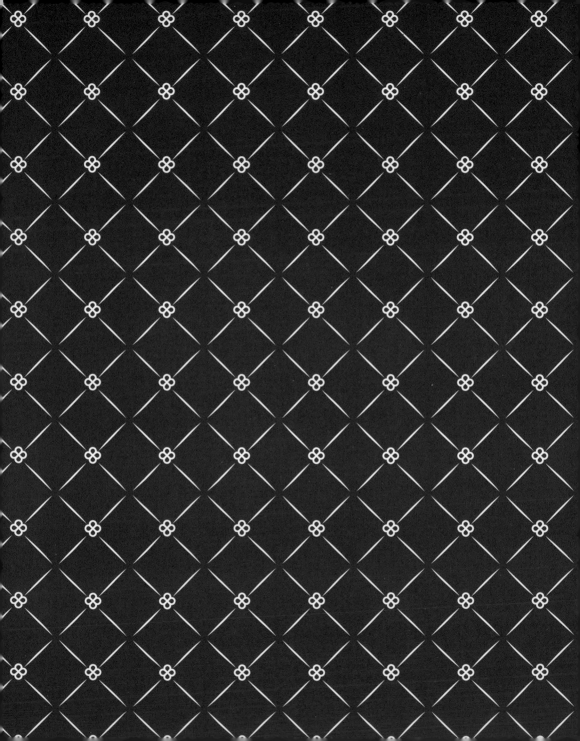

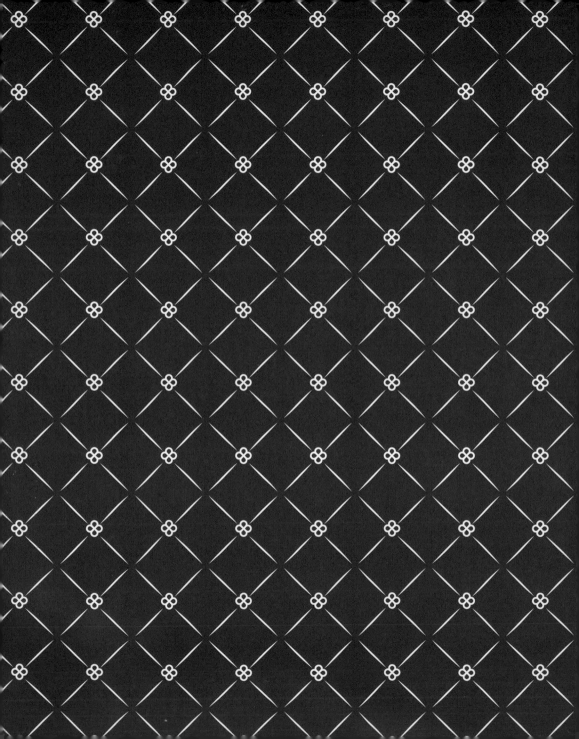